D0235885

The New Adventures of Postman Pat

John Cunliffe

Illustrated by Stuart Trotter

from the original television designs by Ivor Wood

a division of Hodder Headline plc

More Postman Pat adventures:

Postman Pat follows a trail
Postman Pat has the best village

First published 1996
by Hodder Children's Books,
a division of Hodder Headline plc,
338 Euston Road, London NW1 3BH

ISBN 0 340 678089
10 9 8 7 6 5 4 3 2 1

A catalogue record for this book
is available from the British Library.

Printed in Italy.

There was a touch of Spring in the air, in Greendale.

Pat was on his way in his little red van. There was not much post today. Pat stopped to smell the hedgerow blossom. There was a green lane winding up the hillside - just the place for a walk!

“Come on, Jess,” said Pat. “Stretch your paws!”

Over the hill, over a stream, round by a coppice, Pat saw someone he knew.

“Well, look who’s here! Morning, Miss Hubbard!” said Pat.

“Morning, Pat!”

Miss Hubbard was getting ready to paint a picture.

“Just the day for a bit of painting,” said Pat.

A gust of wind sent her picture flying.

"Oh, Pat!" cried Miss Hubbard. "My picture! Quick, catch it!"

Postman Pat ran as fast as he could, and soon spotted the picture, stuck in the hedge.

"It must think it's a boat," said Pat, "sailing away like that. Here we are, Miss Hubbard. All safe."

"Oh, thank you, Pat," said Miss Hubbard. "This is a most important picture for the Garner Bridge Art Show. The *Pencaster Gazette* is offering a prize - you never know, I might win!"

"Well, I never read about that," said Pat. "I've been too busy reading the addresses on my letters to read the paper."

Miss Hubbard put a big splash of paint on the canvas.

"Hmmm, not a bad start!" she said. "What do you think of that?"

Pat wasn't sure.

"Well . . . hmmm . . . I don't . . . erm . . . is it . . .?" he said. "All that yellow - it fair makes you squint!"

The wind blew again. The picture blew off the easel, and smeared paint all down Miss Hubbard's blouse.

"I think that wind's trying to paint you!" said Pat.

"It's no good, Pat . . ." said Miss Hubbard. "I'll have to go home and paint a pot of flowers on the kitchen table."

The wind blew Pat on his way.
There was a parcel for Ted.
"Morning, Ted!"

“Morning, Pat! I hope you’ve got a parcel for me.”

“I have,” said Pat, “and it looks like something special.”

“Special? I should think so!” said Ted. “It’s a thingummy-wotsit for this do-lally gadget I’m making for the Art Show.”

“I thought you had to do a painting?” said Pat.

“This is for the Action-Sculpture section. Modern stuff.”

“Well, I wouldn’t mind having a go,” said Pat, “but I don’t think I could make a do-lally wotsit.”

“Well, there’s all sorts of things you could try . . .” said Ted. “What about a spot of painting? I have plenty of tins with a bit left in; I’d be glad to get them used up.”

“I was watching Miss Hubbard this morning,” said Pat. “It looks a bit messy, specially when that wind gets up.”

Ted showed Pat a small statue.

"You could make a statue like mine - I've got a nice bit of marble - picked it up at a junk shop, last week. You're welcome to use it. I could lend you a hammer and chisel. You'd soon knock something out."

"I'd be more likely to knock my fingers off," said Pat. "Dangerous things, hammers."

"You'd better try something soft, then," said Ted.

"Julian has some nice stuff," said Pat. "All squishy - but I don't think you can make statues out of it."

"What you want is a nice lump of clay. I always say there's nothing like it."

"That sounds more my style," said Pat, "but where could I get such a thing as a lump of clay?"

Ted started rootling about amongst his shelves. "I've got a tin of some special stuff; it's like clay, but it sets hard without going in a kiln. You're welcome to try it, if you like."

"I'll have a go," said Pat.

"You might win a prize!" said Ted.

"But what's this thing that you're making?" said Pat. "How does it work?"

"Now don't tell anybody, Pat. It's to be a secret until the show opens. They've never seen anything like this. It all works with the wind, you see - you need a good breeze to get it going. This fan might do . . . look out!"

The fan made a great whoosh of wind. Bits and pieces blew off Ted's wonderful weather-house, and whirled round the workshop. Pat and Ted ran here and there, trying to catch them. Ted switched the fan off, and all was calm again.

"I'd better be off!" said Pat. "I've had enough wind today to last me for a long time.

"At least this stuff doesn't look windy!" said Pat, as he put the tin of clay in his van.

"What about a clay mouse, Jess? That might do . . ."

Pat was on his way.

The post office was crowded when Pat called in at lunch-time. He said to Mrs Goggins,

"About this Art Show . . . Now then, do you know–?"

"No, Pat, I don't," said Mrs Goggins. "The whole of Greendale's all a-buzz about it, and I'm tired of answering questions.

"Besides, there's a deal of letters to be sorted, so there'll be no time for chatting about the Art Show! Anyway, Pat, you'll not be making a daub for that show, will you?"

"I'm thinking of having a go at something!" said Pat. "Just wait and see!"

It was a quiet evening for Pat. Sara was at the W.I. Julian was doing his homework. Pat had a look at the *Pencaster Gazette*. Then he said,

"Now where did I put that tin?"

He found Ted's tin of clay in the cupboard, and opened the lid.

"Now then, what shall I make?" said Pat. "A model of Jess? First job - get it out of the tin."

Pat tried to read the instructions on the label.

"What does it say? I wish Ted hadn't spilt paint on it. Something about . . . keep warm, and mix a small amount of water . . . take care to . . . Hmmm . . . can't see the rest. Never mind - I'll just see what happens."

He tipped it out on the kitchen table. It went all soft and sloppy. It spread out into a sticky patch, that grew bigger and bigger. Then it began to drip over the edges of the table, and slop on to the floor.

"Oh, dear, now what?"

He ran round the table trying to catch it in the can. It was no good. The moment he caught it in one place, it went oozing somewhere else. A sticky mess of clay spread across the floor! Pat stepped in it, and he was soon covered in clay as well.

Poor Pat! It took him hours to clean it up. When Sara came home, he had to start all over again, as she said she had never seen such a mess in all her days. Pat had to put all his clothes in the washer, and have a bath and a shampoo before he looked even half decent.

The next morning, Pat phoned Ted.

"I had a spot of bother with that clay-stuff you gave me . . . took me till bed-time to clean it up."

"What did you make?" said Ted.

"A mess - that's what I made, Ted - nothing else! You should have heard what Sara said when she came home. I've never known her so cross."

"You have to follow the instructions, Pat, then it's OK. I'll see if I can find a leaflet about it. I know I've got one somewhere."

Greendale would never be the same again. In every house and farm, people were painting, drawing, sewing, modelling and carving like mad, all racing to be ready for the big Art Show.

At the village school, they made a big picture with all the people of Greendale in it.

When Pat called on Miss Hubbard she was busy working on her painting. She said,

"Do you like my picture, Pat? The wind can't get at me here! I call it Still Life With Falling Petals."

"It looks to be getting smaller and smaller," said Pat.

"Well, you see," said Miss. Hubbard, "I'm a slow painter, and the petals fall faster than I paint."

"Well I hope there's something left by the time you finish!" said Pat. "Cheerio!"

At Thompson Ground Pat found Alf trying to peep through the closed curtains of the parlour.

"What do you think, Pat?" said Alf. "Dorothy's shut herself in there, and won't let anybody in."

"What is she up to?" said Pat.

"It's something to do with this Art Show - she's making a great secret of it. Says someone might copy her idea. But look, I found some wool under the table!"

"She might be knitting something." said Pat. "Perhaps it's a tickly winter vest for you, and you'll have to model it at the show! Cheerio!"

There were some letters for Ted.

"Hello, Pat," he said. "I sorted it all out about that clay-stuff. You warm it to make it go soft. Then you sprinkle water on it to make it go hard."

"We had the stove on in our kitchen when I tried it," said Pat. "It must be that that made it go so runny."

When Pat got home, he just had to have another try with that clay. He kept it cool, so it was not runny this time. There it was, a great lump on the table, waiting to be made into something. He wasn't sure what it was going to be.

He pushed it and shaped it with his fingers. He smoothed it and patted it. After a long time, it began to look like something.

"Hmmm, I've seen that somewhere before!" said Pat.

It looked more and more like a cat. One special cat . . . a cat called Jess!

At last, the day of the Art Show came.

All over Greendale, people were travelling towards the village school, where the show was to be held. They came on bikes, on tractors, and in cars. Some just walked. Each one carried something, carefully wrapped,

or tied and taped in a cardboard box - something for the Show.

Pat popped in with his model of Jess, first thing, when he was delivering the letters. Each one hoped to win a prize. The judging was to be at two o'clock that afternoon.

Pat had to go to George Lancaster's with a parcel before he could go to the Show. But his van was making some very peculiar noises. George came to have a look at it.

"What's wrong, Pat?" he said. "I know a thing or two about motors. Let's see if we can fettle it."

Sam Waldron arrived. When he looked inside Pat's van, he knew what was wrong. He said,

"There's nothing wrong with your van, Pat. It's just that it won't run on fresh air! You're out of petrol!"

"Oh, what a noodle I am!" said Pat. "And I'll miss the Art Show! They're picking the winner this afternoon!"

"Here you are," said Sam. "I can spare you a drop - enough to get you down to the village, anyway."

Sam brought a can, and poured some petrol into Pat's van. The van went much better with petrol in it - but not for long! It began to choke and splutter again, and it stopped dead on the edge of the village.

“Come on, Jess,” said Pat. “We’ll have to walk the rest of the way . . . Hurry up, Jess - we might be in time!”

Pat was out of puff when he got to the school. There was no sign of the judge, but a lot of people seemed to be looking at Pat’s model of Jess. There was a notice on it:
SPECIAL AWARD - GREENDALE PRIZE.

The Reverend Timms came bustling up to Pat, saying,

"It's a prize for you, Pat! Your model saved the Show!"

"But how could it?" said Pat. "And - there's - there's something missing - what happened to its tail? It isn't a Manx cat!"

"Don't worry, Pat . . ." said Ted. "Come and look in this cupboard. You see that pipe?"

"Never mind that pipe," said Pat. "My feet are getting wet! Is there a flood?"

"There was a leak," said Ted. "Look . . . that big pipe, down there."

"That's Jess's tail wrapped round the pipe!" said Pat.

"Well, not Jess's," said Sara, laughing.

"Jess's statue's," said Julian.

Ted said, "The cold water makes that clay go hard, so it's just the thing to stop a leak. Without that we would have had to close the Show down."

Jess was sitting next to his model.

"This is the best model of a cat I ever saw!" said Miss Hubbard. "Now let's see - which one is the model?"

Jess looked cross, and arched his back.

"Oh, sorry, Jess. Doesn't he look proud!"

"He's a First Prize cat!" said Pat.
"And he always has been! Well done, Jess!"

"And well done, Pat!" said Miss Hubbard.

And everyone agreed with that.

As for Jess, he went to see if he could find something for his tea. Clay cats were all very well, but he was feeling hungry.